This book belongs to

For James, Connie and Cecily x

ABOUT THE AUTHOR

Susan Hughes lives in Derbyshire with her family and two rescue cats. With a background in primary and early years education, Susan loves to write fun and engaging stories for children and grown-ups to share together which make you laugh, smile or maybe even bring a tear to your eye! Sprout's Surprise is the first in a series of fun escapades to help children make sense of the world around them.

If you enjoy Sprout's Surprise, please do leave a review online. It will help others to find out about the story and it is really appreciated. Thank you for reading and for taking the time!

Visit sproutssurprisebooks.com to join Susan's newsletter about Sprout's adventures and to download free book themed ideas and resources for children and grown-ups to use at home and in the classroom.

Sprout's Surprise

Copyright Susan Hughes 2021

Published by Treacle City Press 2021

All rights reserved.

ISBN: 978-1-8384020-0-6

Treacle City Press

www.treaclecitypress.com

SPROUT'S SURPRISE!

Susan Hughes

Illustrated by Emily May

Sprout was having fun
sliding around,
on a thrown out banana
skin that he had found.

But Sprout didn't know,
as he hadn't yet seen,

that his tummy was starting to turn
bright green!

Sprout **whizzed** up a tin tray resting on bricks, eager to show off his skateboarding tricks.

As he slid off the end, he did a HUGE spin

landing upside down
in the compost bin!

"Poohwee!" gasped Sprout, "what on EARTH is that smell?"

COMPOST BIN

He was covered in **peelings** and bits of eggshell!

Scarecrow held out his hand,

"you better hop out,
before you turn into
compost too, Sprout!"

Climbing out of the bin he was now a bit **smelly**
and THAT's when Sprout saw his bright green belly!

"Goodness!"

gasped Sprout,

"I'm really quite sure, my tummy has
never been this green before!"

Sprout found an
old toothbrush
to scrub himself clean

but the more he
scrubbed, the more
he turned **green!**

The **next day** Sprout searched
the ground near the bin
to skateboard again on the banana skin.

But when he found it lying on the floor
the skin was all black and no good anymore!

"Oh nooooooo!"

? ? cried Sprout, scratching his head,

"What am I going to do now instead?"

Suddenly he spied with his little eye

some boxes and cartons piled up really high.

Sprout had an idea of what he could do,

SHED

"I just need 4 bottle tops, a box and some glue!"

In no time at all,
Sprout had made a
sports car!

And shot past the shed
like a **shooting star!**

As he weaved in and out
of the vegetable row,

all Scarecrow could see was
a **bright green** glow!

"Wow, Sprout!" gasped
Scarecrow, "you are SO green.
You are the greenest Sprout
I've ever seen!"

"My tummy's so green it's starting to glow, but I don't know why?" said Sprout to Scarecrow.

Recycling?" asked Sprout, "what do you mean?"
"And why is my tummy turning so green?"

"Well," smiled Scarecrow, "I scare off the crows

but I can't do that without any clothes!

So instead of throwing
his old clothes out

the farmer dressed me,"
said Scarecrow to Sprout.

"You found new ways to use old things too.
Recycling is something we all can do!"

"Reusing things makes
our world **healthy** and
cleaner
and each time you did,
you became **greener**
and **greener**."

"Wow! I've been recycling
but I never knew!

I love being green.
It's my favourite colour too."

Sprout's tips!

Fun story themed activities for children and grown-ups to do together. Enjoy learning through play as well as being eco-friendly!

- Make some homemade playdough (green of course), then make your very own Sprout!

- Grow a Sprout! Sit a Brussel sprout on the top of a bottle of water (change water daily) and watch its roots grow. What happens if you then plant it in soil?

- Gardening – many vegetables can be regrown from kitchen scraps. Find out which you can regrow and have a go.

- Overripe bananas? Don't throw away - they are perfect to make banana muffins or banana bread! Measure and count out the ingredients together.

- Reuse old clothes and build your own Scarecrow.

- Start making your own compost! Find out what you can/cannot put into it.

- Reuse an empty plastic bottle to make a rain catcher.

- Junk modelling – make your very own sports car or one of your own ideas!

- Make a bird seed feeder for Scarecrow's little bird! Reuse a kitchen roll cardboard tube, cover it all over with lard, roll it in bird seed and hang with string on a tree. Watch the birds feed! How many come to visit? Can you name them?

- Make seed starter pots from upcycled egg cartons, yoghurt pots, polystyrene cups. Reuse plastic bakery cartons for seed trays. Fill with potting compost and sow some seeds. Did you know you can even sow a seed in used tea bags and grow mushrooms in used filter coffee grinds?

- Put recyclable materials (egg cartons, kitchen roll tubes, cereal boxes, plastic bottles etc) in a large plastic tub, tuff tray or sand pit. Add dry material such as rice, pasta, oats or sand with different sized scoops and spoons then just add your imagination!

- Sort junk materials into groups - plastic, cardboard, paper etc. What are they made of? Which can be recycled? Which go in the rubbish bin?

Questions can help children to reflect on and talk about the story and pictures but try not to interrupt the story too often — enjoy it and just choose a few each time you read the book.

Before reading the story (front cover)

- Talk about the front cover together. Can you see any letters of your name in the title? Who is Sprout? A girl? Boy? What do you think the surprise will be?
- What's Sprout doing on the banana skin?

As you read the story:

- Why do you think Sprout's tummy is starting to turn bright green?
- What's a compost bin/compost? What do you put in it?
  Why might Sprout turn into compost?
- Why do you think Sprout's tummy is still turning green as he is scrubbing himself clean? What is he scrubbing himself with?
- What is Sprout standing under to take a shower? Where has the water come from? Why do you think the banana skin turned all black?
- What could Sprout do instead of skateboarding on a banana skin?
- What do you think Sprout is going to do with the box and bottle tops?
- Why do you think Sprout's tummy is glowing?
- What is recycling?
- Can you think of all the things that Sprout reused? (banana skin — skateboard; tin tray and bricks — skateboard ramp; toothbrush — scrubbing brush; rain water from water butt to shower with; cardboard box and bottle tops — sports car)

After reading the story:

- What was Sprout's Surprise? (He had no idea he had been recycling; his tummy turning bright green was also a surprise and a clue; every time he reused something he became greener and greener).
- What do you think 'being green' means?
- What things could you reuse? Can you think of things to recycle?
- What was your favourite part of the story?
- Can you think when Sprout was sad, happy, surprised in the story?
- Can you think of a time when you have been sad, happy or surprised?

ACKNOWLEDGEMENTS

Huge thanks to my illustrator, Emily May, for bringing Sprout and the story to life so wonderfully. Special thanks to Clare Emerick for her unwavering support and advice from when Sprout was just a mere seed in my imagination! Thanks also to author, Dawn Brookes for her invaluable self-publishing advice. Love and thanks also to family, friends and all the nursery school children whose enjoyment and feedback of the story in the early days encouraged me to keep going.

YOU ARE ALL SUPER SPROUTS!

Coming Soon!

You will be hearing more about Sprout's adventures soon! If you would like to hear about new book updates, visit sproutssurprisebooks.com to join my newsletter.

You can also connect with me and follow what Sprout is getting up to on Twitter and Instagram @sproutssurprise.

Sprout's Surprise is perfect to introduce a recycling topic in the classroom and for home learning. For more activity ideas of how the book can be used across all areas of learning in the Early Years Foundation Stage Curriculum, sign up for Sprout's Tips on the website above where you can download free topic planning and other resources.

What will Sprout's
next surprise be...?

Printed in Great Britain
by Amazon